THE
WORLD
MORE
FULL OF
WEEPING

ROBERT J. WIERSEMA

ChiZine Publications

FIRST EDITION, SECOND PRINTING

The World More Full of Weeping © 2009 by Robert J. Wiersema
Jacket artwork © 2009 by Erik Mohr
All Rights Reserved.

LIBRARY AND ARCHIVES CANADA CATALOGUING IN PUBLICATION

Wiersema, Robert J.
The world more full of weeping / Robert J. Wiersema ; editors: Brett
Alexander Savory & Sandra Kasturi.

ISBN 978-0-9809410-8-1 (bound).--ISBN 978-0-9809410-9-8 (pbk.)

I. Savory, Brett Alexander, 1973- II. Kasturi, Sandra, 1966- III. Title.

PS8645.I33W67 2009   C813'.6   C2009-903946-X

CHIZINE PUBLICATIONS
Toronto, Canada
www.chizinepub.com
info@chizinepub.com

Edited by Brett Alexander Savory
Copyedited and proofread by Sandra Kasturi

THE
WORLD
MORE
FULL OF
WEEPING

For Xander,
who may not have a forest,
but is walking a path of his own.

And for Cori,
because the principles of magic remain.

F or breakfast on the morning of the day he disappeared, Brian Page ate most of two scrambled eggs, three pieces of bacon, and almost two slices of multigrain toast. After he was gone, his father, Jeff Page, kept remembering the remaining triangle of hardening bread on its plate on the kitchen counter, the outline of Brian's bite sharp, a bright curve against the right angle.

It wasn't just the food that Jeff remembered from that morning: it was the conversation. It was what his eleven-year-old son had said the last time they had spoken.

"Your mom called last night," Jeff had said. "After you were asleep." He was standing at the stove, cracking four eggs into a skillet glazed slick with bacon grease.

Brian was at the table, munching at a strip of bacon from the platter. He didn't say anything.

"She said she'd be here at four to pick you up." He scrambled the eggs in the pan, breaking the yolks with the edge of the flipper, then turning the mass over, folding it in on itself, the yolk first marbling the white then dissipating entirely.

"Bring me over your plate," he said, lifting the pan off the heat. He scraped about half the four eggs onto his son's plate, then dumped the remainder onto his own and sat down at the table across from him.

"Do I have to go?" Brian asked quietly.

Jeff swallowed a mouthful. "What?"

"I just . . . Do I really have to go to Mom's this week?"

"We've talked about this. Your mom's really . . . what's up, bud?"

Brian shrugged and looked down at his plate.

"Is there a problem? Did something happen at your mom's place?" It was stupid, he knew, but his mind went immediately to Bill, Diane's new boyfriend. It was the way parents were wired to think, now.

Brian shook his head. "No, it's nothing like that. I'd just really like to stay here this week."

More than anything, Jeff wanted to give Brian his way. He wasn't looking forward to the week on his own, and to what it portended, and if Brian wanted to stay with him more than he wanted to visit his mother, wasn't that the important thing?

Instead, he said, "We've talked about this, bud. There's a lot of stuff to plan, and this is how it works out best."

"Doesn't work out best for me," he said, with the glum petulance only an eleven-year-old can muster.

"What's this about?" Jeff asked, leaning toward his son.

"Nothing." He pushed his eggs around his plate.

"Your mom's got a big week planned. I think she wants to take you to Science World and the aquarium, and maybe to the movies as well as showing you the school. . . . It sounds like she's really looking forward to hanging out with you. Doesn't that sound good?"

Brian took a mouthful of eggs.

"Brian, what's going on? Did you and your mom have a fight?" He was surprised he hadn't heard anything about this before. Diane was usually good at monitoring and reporting any problems. "Is there something you want to talk to me about?"

"You wouldn't get it," he said into his plate. "Why can't I just stay here?"

Jeff wanted to lean forward and touch his son, ruffle his hair or pull him close, but he knew better. "I know it's tough, bud. It's not easy for any of us."

"I knew you wouldn't understand." He picked up a forkful of eggs, muttering, "Carly said you wouldn't understand."

"Understand what?" Jeff asked. "Tell me. Tell me and I'll try. I really will."

Brian shook his head, and took a bite out of a piece of bacon he held between his thumb and forefinger as an uneasy silence settled over the kitchen.

Carly said you wouldn't understand.

Were those really the last words his son had spoken to him?

Over the next few days of men in hip waders and pick-up trucks, of CB radios and low-flying helicopters, Jeff would struggle to remember something else—anything else— Brian might have said. Did he really not say anything for the remainder of breakfast? Or while he was getting ready to go out to the woods? He was mad; it was possible he was giving his father the silent treatment. Likely, in fact.

Had he even acknowledged that he had heard Jeff tell him to be home by 3:30 for his mom? Jeff remembered him turning and looking back at him as he went upstairs, but did that mean he had heard? Or was he just looking back: defiant, unhappy, misunderstood?

Carly said you wouldn't understand.

Jeff was in his shop when he heard the sound of gravel crunching in the driveway and the familiar engine. He stepped to the open door in time to see Diane's Explorer pull to a stop between the shop and the back porch. He raised a hand in greeting, then grabbed a rag to clean up.

"Working pretty hard for a Sunday," Diane said as she crossed the yard toward him.

He shrugged. "The work's always there. Figured I might as well."

"And what are you elbow-deep in today?" she asked, coming to a stop less than an arm's length from him.

He had to think for a moment: she had a knack for disarming him with nothing more than her presence. It had always been that way between them, but it had gotten worse since she had moved out. Times like this, with her looking so pretty and well-scrubbed, practically shining in the afternoon light, made it difficult for him to even think.

12

"A re-build for Frank Kelly."

"Nothing too challenging, then." She smiled at him, and it felt for a moment like they were flirting.

"Could do it with my eyes closed," he said, without a hint of bragging. "How was the drive?"

She shrugged. "Two hours on the freeway. Could do it with my eyes closed."

He smiled.

The argument that had ended their marriage had, in fact, grown out of their very first disagreement. It had started as a conversation seventeen years before, and had played through the intervening time like background music to every disagreement between them.

Seventeen years before, she had said it as if there had been no question: "You don't really want to stay here."

They had been sitting at the table in his father's kitchen—this kitchen—drinking the day's first cup of coffee after their first night together in the house where he had grown up. The house where he now lived with their son, though not for much longer.

"What do you mean?"

She had looked at him as if she didn't understand the question. He knew the feeling.

It wasn't the first time they had seemed to be coming from different worlds.

They had both been going to school, BCIT in Vancouver. Jeff was qualifying for his apprenticeship, and Diane had been taking some introductory broadcasting classes. They had met at a party; Jeff didn't even know how he had ended up there, standing alone in the corner with a warm beer.

She had rescued him by swooping in and dancing him away. That was the way she saw it, at least.

It had been three months before he brought her home for the weekend, to meet and be met.

"Why would I go anywhere else?" he had asked in response to her question.

She had shaken her head. "There's a whole world to see out there. So much more than this." She had gestured around her, at the kitchen, the house, the town. His world.

If she had been at all mean, at all disparaging, it would have been over right then. But there had been no trace of haughtiness, no condescension. She was trying to rescue him again, he understood.

It hadn't worked.

"You made good time," he said, tossing his rag onto his workbench. "You're early."

She glanced at her watch and shook her head.

He turned sharply to glance at the shop clock. 4:20.

"I even tried calling to say I was going to be a little late."

Four-twenty. Later, he would wonder where the time had gone. How he had gotten so involved in a simple engine rebuild that he had lost track of the hours? Had lost track of Brian?

"He's probably in the house," he said, gesturing toward the back porch. "I told him to be back by 3:30 to get cleaned up for you."

But Brian wasn't in the house.

Brian had first met Carly several weeks before, early on a Saturday morning.

His dad had still been asleep when Brian had gotten up. He had moved around the house as quietly as he could, dressing, going to the bathroom, loading his knapsack. At a time when most of the kids from school would be settling in front of the TV for a morning of cartoons, Brian poured a large measure of Cheerios into a plastic sandwich bag and crammed it into his jacket pocket. Pulling on his boots, he let himself out the back door and set out across the field for the woods.

Just behind the old barn, the spaces between the trees were pretty clear: it was easy to walk through, easy to find a place to sit and munch on a handful of cereal. The air was bright and clear, filled with the sound of birds. From where he sat, Brian could look out at the back of his father's shop, the backyard, the house, and the road beyond it. The whole time he was sitting there, he didn't see a single car pass.

Farther back into the woods, it grew darker and quieter. He zipped up his coat against the chill. After he crossed the old fence-line, Brian stayed close to the few beaten trails. Off the paths, the undergrowth was thick and tough. It changed, too, depending on where he was in the woods. Sometimes he would be in the midst of a swollen, twisted stand of blackberry vines. Other times he'd pull his arms in to avoid the trunks and branches of a patch of devil's club, the spines of which would pierce you right through your clothes, bury themselves deep in your skin and keep working their way in.

Deeper in the woods, it was almost silent. What birds there were flew quietly and alone. The loudest sounds were Brian's breath, the scrunch of his boots on the earth, and the rustle of leaves or branches that he pushed out of his way with a stick.

Sometimes he heard a scrambling in the underbrush as an animal dodged away. When this happened, he would stop, stand stock-still and listen, his eyes following his ears as he tried to find the animal, to see what kind it was.

He was never scared, only curious, and he could wait, motionless, for an eternity, just for a glimpse of something wild. He wasn't disappointed if it turned out to be a squirrel—he loved squirrels—but he treasured the memory of the day he saw the yellow eyes of the coyote looking at him through the bramble, the time he had come upon the family of raccoons at play in the dimming of the late afternoon, the day he thought he had seen a bear, the crashing in the underbrush too long and too loud to have been caused by anything smaller.

He hadn't told his father about the bear.

He didn't tell his father much about his days in the woods. It wasn't that his father wouldn't understand: he knew some of the trails he walked had been cut by his father and his uncles when they were boys. And it wasn't that he was afraid he would be reined in, that the revelation he had seen a bear—maybe—would result in him being kept to the yard or the open early woods where the cows used to graze. That thought hadn't even occurred to him.

No, he didn't talk about the woods because to talk about them would have meant sharing them.

The woods were something that belonged to Brian, a rare thing he didn't have to share, a rare place where he could truly be himself, where he could watch the slow progress of bugs along a branch, or study the skeletal webbing on the underside of a leaf. A place where he didn't have to explain himself to anyone, where he didn't have to pretend to be anyone else.

The woods were his world, and his alone.

Until the moment Carly stepped out of the brush by the creek and raised her hand in greeting.

"Hello?"

Jeff struggled to keep the worry out of his voice, speaking loudly to be sure the old man on the other end of the phone line would be able to hear. "John? It's Jeff from up the road." He looked at Diane as he said the words, but she was staring out the kitchen window, out at the woods, and she hadn't even heard. "I was just wondering—have you seen Brian at all today? He went out into the woods a few hours ago and I was expecting him back."

He and Diane had come into the house together, expecting to see Brian at the table with a sandwich, or to hear him crashing around in his room, belatedly packing for his week away. As soon as they stepped through the door, though, they knew he wasn't there: the house felt empty, cold, and silent.

When they called out his name, it was more to puncture the quiet around them than in any hope that he might answer.

"I haven't seen him, Jeff. Not today. Sometimes he comes out back of the house here and Claire'll give him a hot chocolate and some cookies before he heads for home, but I haven't seen him today."

Jeff felt a door closing within himself. "Thanks, John. I'll—"

"How long's he been gone for?" John's voice was thin and brittle, but still strong. John Joseph had the voice of a man who was used to being listened to, who never needed to shout to be heard.

Diane stepped away from the window and looked at him.

"I'm not entirely sure," he confessed. "I got caught up in some work and I didn't notice the time."

"That's probably exactly what happened with your boy, too. Got caught up in what he was doin'."

"Like father like son," Jeff muttered.

John chuckled drily. "Not the first time that's been said. At any rate, it's probably too early to be worried. I'll take a wander out the back and see if I can spot him."

"Thanks, John." Just talking with the older man had helped blunt the knife-edge of panic in his stomach.

"And you tell that ex-wife of yours we say hello, all right?"

Jeff smiled. Not much escaped his neighbours' notice. John and Claire Joseph mostly kept to themselves, but they seemed to have the blood of the whole town running in their veins. "Will do, John. You take care." He was about to say goodbye when he remembered. "Hey, actually, John, do you know of anyone in the area, any of the kids, named Carly?"

"Carly?"

"Yeah. I didn't recognize the name but I thought you might know if her family had just moved here. Brian's mentioned her a couple of times over the last few weeks."

"Carly," the old man repeated, as if leafing through his memory.

"Probably about Brian's age. Ten or eleven maybe. I think he's been playing with her in the woods."

"Jeff." This time there was no thinness to the voice, not even a hint of age. "I think it might be best if you call Chuck Minette at the Search and Rescue. I think it might be best that you call him right now."

The day they first met, Brian didn't hear Carly so much as sense her presence behind him.

He was hunched over the still backwater of Russell Creek, leaning forward with one of his tools to take a sample of the green slime that clung to the edges of the pond. The rock he was leaning on was rough and cold, and he huffed as he stretched himself as far as he could, but he got the sample.

When he straightened up, rubbing the rock indentations on his palm with his other hand, he felt a wave of cold run through him, a nervous certainty that he was not alone.

"Hello?" he called, his voice barely raised, as he glanced around the clearing. There was no one there.

A light breeze rustled in the branches around the still pond.

He felt someone's eyes upon him.

"Dad?" he called, rising slowly to his feet. The sample spoon dangled limply by his side.

"Hello?"

He turned in a slow circle, taking in all of the clearing as he thought of the stories in the books he had read. Stories about bear attacks, and what would happen if a wolf pack got you. Or worse. The stories of crazy people who took little boys like him out to the woods where no one would hear them—

"Hello?" he called again, his voice cracking. "Is anybody there?"

"I'm here," came a soft voice from the tree line behind him. A girl's voice.

He turned quickly, almost losing his balance.

She stepped from the path into the clearing without a sound. "I'm sorry," she said, raising her hand in a half-wave. "I didn't mean to scare you. I'm Carly."

As she stepped toward him, she smiled.

You never really get a look at your own life, Jeff Page thought, *until you're showing it to someone else.*

Dean Owens was the first of the Search and Rescue to arrive, parking his truck under the cedar tree at the side of the driveway. As he climbed out of the cab, he straightened his ball cap and grabbed a metal clipboard.

Jeff nodded as he approached. "Thanks for getting here so fast."

"I was on duty. The rest of the crew should be along pretty quick. How you holdin' up?"

Jeff glanced over at Diane. His wife—*ex-wife*, he reminded himself—stared at the edge of the woods like she could will Brian to reappear. Her arms were folded tightly across her chest, her jacket zipped to her throat against a chill that wasn't coming from outside. "We're pretty worried. It's gonna be getting dark soon."

"Okay," Dean said. "Let's get this out of the way." He opened the metal folio and clicked a pen to start.

As they ran through Brian's distinguishing characteristics, Diane drifted soundlessly, wordlessly toward them.

"And when did you last see him?"

"Maybe eleven this morning. I was working."

"And you're sure he went off into the woods?"

Jeff nodded.

"And you've checked with all of his friends? Maybe he's over at one of their places."

Jeff glanced at Diana. "He doesn't . . . he's pretty much a loner. He's mentioned a girl, Carly, a few times, but I don't know her last name."

"We'll look into it," Dean said, making a note. "Did you have a fight or argument recently?"

Jeff was startled by the question. "Why? What does that—" He glanced at Diana, who was staring at him.

"We're just trying to determine if maybe he ran away. Maybe there was a fight, or some punishment . . ."

"Brian wouldn't run away," Diane said. Her first words in more than half an hour were calm, but there was an edge of fear under them.

Dean looked at her. "You'd be surprised at the number of kids we end up rescuing from the video store or the arcade in town 'cause they were pissed off at their parents. Husbands and wives, too," he added, looking between them and trying to lighten the mood.

"There was a fight," Jeff said quietly. "This morning. Brian didn't—he asked if he had to go to his mom's place in Vancouver this week. He wanted to stay home." He avoided looking at Diane as he recounted their breakfast conversation, but he could feel the force of her stare.

"Is that it?" Dean asked. "He just didn't want to go on vacation in the city?"

"No," Diane said flatly. "We . . . He's going to be moving in with me in the summer. Starting school in Vancouver in the fall. He didn't want to—doesn't want to . . ."

Dean stared at Diane for a moment, then back at Jeff. He pursed his lips as he made another note on the clipboard.

Jeff willed himself not to look at his ex-wife.

"So what can you tell me about the woods?" Dean asked, breaking the awkward silence.

"You probably remember," Jeff started, finally daring a glance at Diane. She had turned away, and was staring at the ground. He recognized the biting of her lower lip, the way she tried to keep from crying. "It hasn't changed much."

When they were younger, Jeff and Dean and a bunch of the other kids used to rule the woods behind the house, building forts out of hollow trees, waging war on one another, and building traps for anyone who might come looking for them.

Dean half-smiled. "I've been in a lot of forests since then," he said. "They really do all start to look the same."

Jeff felt fleetingly chastised as he turned toward the forest. The air was dimming, growing heavy and thick as the sun touched the horizon behind them.

"We've got about twenty-five acres." He gestured. "From fence line to fence line. But the woods keep going, down past John and Claire's place that way, past young Tom's over there. There's an old fence marking the property line on both ends of our share. Brian's not supposed to cross the fence."

Dean looked at him dubiously.

"Yeah." Jeff shook his head. "And the fence was in pretty bad shape the last time I checked."

In the quiet afternoon distance he heard an engine. Engines.

"And how far back does it go?"

"All the way," Diane answered, almost in a whisper.

"There's an old logging road a ways back," Jeff clarified. "But after that, it meets up with the bush at the foot of the mountain." His voice trailed off. "Brian's not supposed to cross the logging road."

Diane looked at him.

"He knows that."

She shook her head.

"He wouldn't."

There was a crunching of gravel under wheels as the trucks turned into the driveway.

"Here they are," Dean said, turning away.

"Hi." Brian smiled back, a little awkwardly. Not only was he surprised to have someone else in his own private world, he felt a bit shy talking to girls at the best of times. "I'm Brian."

He didn't know if he should try to shake her hand or what.

"What are you doing?" she asked, stepping closer to him.

"Collecting samples," he said, as if it should have been obvious. He was a bit confused by how she was dressed: her long, dark dress didn't seem too suited for tramping around in the woods. "Do you live around here?" he asked, thinking that she reminded him of the Dutch girls from the bigger farms he had seen walking to the Christian school from the bus window, all of them wearing grey dresses, their heads covered with white cloths. She didn't have anything on her head, but Carly had that same old-fashioned look, the same pale skin.

"No, I'm just staying here for a while. What do you do with your samples?"

He remembered the long spoon in his left hand. "Here, I'll show you."

Leaning against the mossy side of a fallen tree, Brian unzipped his backpack and pulled out the wooden case. He set it on the log and flipped open the catches.

"What's that?" Carly asked, looking over his shoulder.

"It's a microscope," he said, setting it mostly flat on the log. "My dad gave it to me. It's pretty old."

"What do you do with it?"

"I'll show you," he repeated. He slid a slide from the package and prepared it with a drop of the scummy water. He moved quickly and confidently: he'd been doing this for several months. He'd broken a few slides at first, but he'd gotten the hang of it. "Then you just slip it in here," he muttered, mostly to himself, as he positioned the slide under the lens. "And you adjust the mirror . . ." Looking through the lens, he adjusted the focus. "There." He stepped to one side, still holding the microscope. "You look."

Holding back her long blonde hair, Carly leaned over the microscope. She looked for a moment, squinting her eyes, then straightened up.

"What is that?" she asked, her face wide and open. "What did you do?"

He had to suppress a laugh. "It's water," he said. "Just a

drop of water from the pond." He gestured.

"But there are things . . . creatures." She seemed to be drawing away from the microscope.

He nodded. "They *are* creatures," he said. "That's what . . . They live in there."

Her face slowly broke into a smile. "They must be very small," she said.

"The microscope magnifies them so we can see them."

She looked at the microscope with what he thought was curiosity.

"Do you want to look again?"

She stepped forward slowly and bent over the microscope. "How did you find them?" she asked. "How did you know they would be there?"

"They're everywhere," he said, excited to be talking about it. "They're all around us. Inside us. In the air and the water."

"Everywhere?"

He nodded.

"Then why haven't I ever seen them?"

"There's a whole world of them, a whole universe, all around us. Just because you can't see them doesn't mean they're not there."

When she looked away from the eyepiece, she was smiling. "Is this what you do in the woods?" she asked.

He nodded, suddenly shy, suddenly unsure of his decision to show the girl his microscope.

"Do you want to see more hidden things, Brian?" she asked. "I could show you. There's a whole hidden world in this forest I could show you, if you wanted."

The first truck parked behind Dean's. People spilled from the cab and cargo bed, mostly men, but a couple of women, too.

Jeff knew everyone, at least in passing. Frank and Jim from the Henderson Press hopped out of the truck's bed, along with Michelle Coombs and Phil Hardie. They drifted over to form a group around Dean.

Moving more slowly, Charlie Ellroy slid from the cab of the truck and walked toward Jeff. He extended a hand, a formality Jeff found oddly disconcerting. He shook it anyway.

"Been a while since we seen you in at the Horseshoe," Charlie said, shifting his mouth around his false teeth.

Jeff nodded. "I've been pretty busy with Brian since . . ." He trailed off as Diane stepped toward them.

"Hi, Charlie," she said.

"How you holdin' up?"

She shrugged, and Jeff could see how much the façade of calm was costing her.

"So you got a little boy lost," he said to Jeff.

"Yeah. Looks that way."

"Like father like son."

It was the second time that cliché had been used that afternoon, and something about it niggled at the back of Brian's mind. He was about to ask Charlie what he meant when a second truck pulled into the driveway.

"That'll be the cloggers," Charlie muttered, watching the driveway.

The truck was driven by Pieter TeBrink, Martin TeBrink's oldest son, now probably in his late twenties, and was loaded with men who looked like they might have been brothers or cousins. All shared the same straight blond hair, the strong chins and white teeth, the broad smiles. TeBrinks and VanLeeuwens, VanderPols and VanWycks. Scions of the Dutch farmers who owned most of the land surrounding Henderson, all wearing the same battered jeans and boots, well worn from use.

Dean drifted toward them as they climbed out of the truck, and the men gravitated to him. Some of them glanced toward Jeff, but none returned his raised hand in greeting.

The Dutch farmers, whose families had been among the first to settle the valley, mostly kept to themselves. They had their own church, their own meeting hall, their own school for their kids. They mostly kept clear of town politics, though Jan VanderWyck was a councilman serving his second term. Most times, people only saw them at the Harvest Festival, where one of their number was usually crowned Harvest King.

Jeff was grateful to see them.

"Friendly," Diane muttered.

"They're all just tryin' to keep their distance." Charlie turned to face them. "In case . . ." His voice trailed off and he looked to the ground. "In case something goes wrong."

The words fell like a hammer on Jeff's heart. For the first time, he had a sense of the real stakes.

He realized he had not felt like there was a real problem.

He had been expecting Brian to rustle out of the woods looking sheepish, having lost track of the time.

Like father, like son.

For the first time, he felt like that might not happen.

"Okay, everyone muster up," Dean called. The Search and Rescue team formed a loose knot around him—everyone except Charlie.

"We don't have much time before dark, so we're gonna hustle out before the truck gets here. We're gonna split into two teams. First team is going to start here. Your search perimeter is due north, between the east and west fence lines. Second team is going to start out on the logging access road and work south between the same two fence lines."

Jeff turned away from the briefing, looked toward the woods, starting to blur and darken in the slow-dimming light.

He felt Diane step up next to him.

"He's going to be all right," he said, without looking at her.

She didn't say anything.

After a moment, he heard the briefing start to break up. He turned away to find Dean writing on his clipboard.

"What team should I be on?" he asked without waiting for him to finish his writing.

Dean looked up at him and shook his head. "The home team," he said slowly, then shook his head more decisively when he saw Jeff start to argue. "No, really. I need you here. I need you close to the phone in case he calls. I need you close to Charlie and the radios in case something comes up. I need you here."

"And you don't want me out there." Jeff said the words flatly, without emotion.

Dean pinched his lips into something that could have passed for a smile. "If it were my son out there, Charlie'd have me waiting by the phone."

"Right." Jeff looked at the ground. Helpless.

Dean touched him on the forearm. "You've got a lot of good people out there, Jeff."

"Right," he said again, and Jeff turned away.

In the distance, he heard boots on gravel, doors opening and closing, hushed voices. Somewhere, an engine started. Somewhere, tires crunched on gravel.

That was another world, though. In his, Jeff was completely alone, still and powerless, as the evening started down.

"Where are we going?" Brian asked, clutching his knapsack tightly as he followed the girl he had just met through the tangled underbrush.

"You'll see," she said, always a couple of steps ahead.

He kept one arm up near his face, sweeping branches away, careful to avoid snapback. The sticks and brambles were thick, and seemed to twist around his feet and legs. "Dammit," he muttered, liking the way the curse sounded.

She moved effortlessly through the rough thicket, slipping between the branches and brambles rather than moving them aside. No curses, no snapbacks, no tripping.

"Are we almost there?" he asked, trying to make it sound like a joke.

"Hush," she said in a stern whisper. She stopped and turned back to him, making a show of pressing her fingers to her lips. "You'll never see anything if you keep making such noise."

"Okay," he whispered, nodding, feeling a little chagrined. "Is it much farther?"

Her smile was bright, and she shook her head. "No. We're here." She beckoned him forward and held her hand out to him.

He stepped up beside her and took her hand like it was the most natural thing in the world. "What?" he asked.

"Look." She cocked her head forward. "Listen."

He leaned forward, conscious of her next to him, of the warmth of her hand in his. He gently pulled aside the brambles, listening hard, trying to filter out the sound of his breathing, the beating of his heart.

He thought he heard something—something small and quiet. He couldn't see anything, just a clutter of brown and green, leaves and branches, and rich, loamy-brown cover on the ground and—

There.

The coyotes were almost the same sandy brown colour as the ground. If he hadn't slowed to look, he wouldn't have seen them. If he hadn't quieted, he would have woken them and they would have slipped away, unseen and unknown.

He was suddenly acutely aware of how much poorer his

life would have been had he never seen them.

It was a mother with three, no, four pups, piled in a loose pack of slumbering brown fur. He was close enough that he could have reached out and touched them. He smelled the rich, feral wildness of them, saw the faint patterns in their fur.

"Wow," he breathed.

A few feet away, the mother coyote's eyes opened, bright yellow against the blurry brown.

Brian froze.

"It's all right," Carly whispered, squeezing his hand. "Stay still."

He felt the coyote's eyes upon him, tracing him, measuring him. There was a depth to the yellow eyes, to the dark pupils, a caution and an understanding. When their eyes met, it was as if something passed between them.

I won't hurt you, he tried to say, without using his voice.

The coyote languidly licked her chops, sighed and shifted herself within the pile of her brood. She closed her eyes slowly, not looking away from Brian.

Carly pulled gently at his hand.

He waited until they were a good distance away before he exploded. "Holy cow, that was amazing! Did you see her? Did you see her looking at me?"

Carly smiled at his excitement. "I saw her."

"At first I was scared. When she opened her eyes, I thought she was—I thought she would protect her cubs. But she just looked at me."

"She could tell you weren't a threat. She knew you

wouldn't hurt her or her children."

"That was so *cool*! How did you know she would be there?"

For a moment, Carly didn't say anything. "There are trails and paths that the animals use. You can follow them if you look closely enough."

Brian's eyes were wide, the rush of excitement thrumming in his veins. His hands shook.

She smiled at his reaction. "Would you like to see more?"

He nodded. "Please."

She took his hand again and led him away.

One of the ways you could tell that someone had spent most of their life in Henderson was by how they approached someone's house.

Diane would always go to front door, ring the bell, then wait.

Most people would go around the back and knock.

John and Claire Joseph, though, just opened the back screen door half an hour after the teams had spread out to start the search, Claire calling "Hello?" up the stairs.

Jeff had been standing at the sink, looking out the window at the people moving through the fields, disappearing into the woods. He turned in time to see Diane stand up from her place at the table and step toward the doorway. She had been sitting at the table, staring into the middle distance, her hands in front of her.

Claire Joseph climbed the stairs slowly, gripping the wooden rail. She was old—Jeff wasn't sure just how old, but he guessed in her eighties—but her eyes were bright and warm.

At the top of the stairs she drew Diane in for an embrace, clutching her tightly without saying a word. When she stepped away, she held onto both of Diane's hands, looked deep into her face.

Tears streamed down Diane's face, and Claire nodded. "That's right. You need to get that out. You're wound up tight as an old watch-spring." She looked over at Jeff, and he tried to smile. "Let's get you cleaned up," Claire said, leading Diane gently down the hallway.

Jeff watched his ex-wife disappear into the bathroom, the door clicking closed behind them.

"I brought over our big coffeemaker," John Joseph said from the foot of the stairs. He was hanging up his coat, several plastic grocery bags at his feet. "And some of Claire's cookies. I thought we might make up some sandwiches as well."

Jeff stepped partway down the stairs and John passed him the bag containing the coffee tureen.

"I didn't hear the truck," he said as they climbed the stairs.

John shook his head. "We walked across the field. Your driveway looked pretty busy."

"Thanks for bringing all this stuff," Jeff said as he

unpacked the bag on the kitchen counter, plugged the cord into the base of the tureen. "It never occurred to me."

"Your mind's on other things." John took a couple of cookie tins from the other bag and set them on the opposite counter.

"Yeah."

John looked out the window over the sink. "We're getting into the gloaming now." He turned to Jeff. "Twilight."

"They won't be able to see too much out there."

"They've got lights. Good ones."

"Yeah." In the window, the world was gradually disappearing, being replaced by his distorted reflection.

Carly walked Brian to the edge of the forest, where the undergrowth was thin and the paths were clear.

She hadn't said anything since he told her that he needed to be getting home. Even in the perpetual shadows of the deepest woods he could tell it was getting late.

"I'll come back tomorrow, though," he said, thinking back on the day they had spent together, and ahead to Sunday morning. There was no other way he would rather spend the hours.

Her face brightened at that.

"Where should we meet?"

They had walked in silence through the forest. It was strange: if anyone had asked him that morning, Brian would have told them that he knew the woods as well as he knew his own house. Better, maybe. But Carly knew paths he had never noticed, knew clearings and fallen trees and swamps bright with skunk cabbage he hadn't even known existed. With her, the woods, which had always seemed comfortable and familiar, seemed to grow, to take on a wondrous strangeness, a foreignness that was kind of unsettling, but mostly thrilling.

As they walked, he wondered if he would have been able to find his way out without her help.

They were no longer holding hands, and as they walked, Brian picked a few wildflowers, careful to be looking away from her when she slowed.

He was surprised that such a short walk—no more than a few minutes—brought them to the tree line between the forest and the fields. He would have thought they were miles away.

"Did you want to come in with me?" he asked, desperate for something to breach the silence between them. "You could probably stay for dinner."

She shook her head, but she smiled. "I should probably be getting back, too."

"Okay," he said, suddenly unsure of himself, not wanting to leave her.

"But you'll come tomorrow?"

He nodded. "Meet you right here?"

She smiled.

He turned away, started to walk, then turned back jerkily. "Here," he said, his face reddening as he extended the flowers to her. "These are for you."

She took them with a smile and a warm glow in her eyes. As she smelled them, he turned away, walking briskly across the field toward his father's shop.

He didn't look back.

His thoughts were filled with excuses, possible scenarios he could use to explain to his father how late he was. It never occurred to Brian to just tell him the truth. He didn't know why.

It didn't matter anyway. When he got to the shop, his father was deep in his work, his eyes tight on the tools but his mind far away.

It was as if he hadn't even noticed his son had been gone.

"You don't get out there much, do you?"

Jeff wasn't startled by John Joseph's voice beside him: the older man had crossed the back lawn without a sound, but Jeff had heard the screen door close.

When he turned toward him, John offered him a mug. "I took a little liberty with the bottle on your counter."

The steam above the mug smelled of coffee and Jameson's. "Thanks."

They both turned their attention to the forest. It was darker now, and Jeff could hear voices coming gradually closer to his farm.

"They'll be coming to get their night gear," John said. "Dean'll probably have the truck stop at the back first, get them set up before he comes back here."

Jeff nodded, not really listening, and took a sip of his coffee. "That's nice," he said, as it warmed him all the way down. "Thanks."

"You don't, do you?" John said, not looking away from the dark forest.

"What?"

"Go out in the woods much." He turned to face Jeff. "'Least not too deep."

"I used to take Brian for walks back there, before he was old enough to go on his own."

John nodded thoughtfully. "Always stayed in sight of the farm, though, I'm guessing."

Jeff shrugged. "I guess. I don't really like being out there too far. Not my sort of place."

John looked at him, the beginnings of a smile seeming to teeter at the corners of his mouth. "It sure used to be. Back when you were Brian's age, you practically lived in the woods."

"I played there a bit."

"It was more than that. Your father was always chasing after you in there, making sure you weren't hung up somewhere, making sure you weren't late for dinner. You spent the winter you were nine or ten planning a camp back there for the next summer. Not a camping trip—a camp. You were gonna spend the summer living back there. You had it all figured out."

Something tickled again at the back of Jeff's mind, a sense of displaced familiarity that allowed him—no, forced him—to concede to John's words. "I guess. I don't remember that at all." He took another sip of his coffee.

The older man had turned his gaze back to the dark, to the rising voices. "I'm not surprised. Not after what happened."

"After what happened?" The tickle was stronger, and he knew what John was going to tell him without actually remembering.

Like father like son.

John turned back to him. "You really don't remember." He didn't seem at all surprised.

"I—"

"That spring, the spring you were eleven years old, you disappeared. You were gone overnight. Almost two days."

Jeff looked at him incredulously. He knew the words were true—though he wasn't sure of just how he knew—but he couldn't help feel that they were referring to someone else. He couldn't make the words match up to his own life.

"Two days."

John nodded. "And a night between. Everyone in town was looking for you. There was no Search and Rescue in those days, but once word got out . . ." He gestured back at the house. "Your mom and Claire made sandwiches and coffee. Kept everyone going."

Like father like son.

"I don't understand how I could forget something like that."

Turning his head sharply, John pointed at the barn. "They're coming out."

The halogen lights of the supply truck swept down the driveway, blinding the men, fixing them in a pool of brightness in the midst of the gaining dark.

The thought came to Brian as he was on the edge of sleep after his first day with Carly. It forced his eyes open, and he felt his heart jump.

We didn't say when we would meet.

Everything about his last few minutes with Carly had been so strange—her silence, the flowers—that he hadn't even thought about setting a time for their meeting the next morning.

It filled him with a sinking sense of dread: what if they missed each other? What if she came and he wasn't there? Would she wait? For how long? Or would she just give up and assume he wasn't coming?

The questions kept circling in his head. The thought of missing Carly, of maybe not seeing her, filled him with a sadness he had never felt before.

That Saturday had been one of the best days of his life. He had never met anyone like Carly before: someone who loved the woods as much as he did. Someone who experienced the same wonder, the same sense of magic, that he did.

Most other people, when he brought up the woods,

would smirk and laugh (if they were other kids) or smile thinly and indulgently as they pretended to listen (if they were grown-ups). Nobody understood what the forest meant to him.

Nobody except Carly.

He couldn't miss her, he just couldn't. How could he have been so stupid, not telling her a time? She was going to get there and not see him and—

He'd just have to get there first. That was it. That was the answer. He'd be out at the edge of the woods as early as he could be, and when she got there, *he* would be waiting for *her*.

He fell asleep moments later with that thought in his mind and a broad smile on his face.

That night, Brian slept the sort of sleep adults envy: rich and deep and dark. The sort of sleep that eleven-year-old boys who spend their days tramping through the woods and playing in streams take for granted, the sort of sleep from which nothing would wake him.

Jeff found Diane in Brian's bedroom, sitting on his bed. She was rubbing her hands together compulsively, folding and twisting them around one another. The room was dark, the flashing yellow lights of the Search and Rescue trucks out the window reflected on her face.

He stood in the doorway in silence, just watching her.

"What did they say?" she asked in a near-whisper, without turning toward him.

He was startled by the sound of her voice. "What?"

"I saw you out there, talking to them."

"They're going back out," he said, stepping into the room. "They've got their lights and radios now." He stopped beside her. He wanted to sit next to her on the bed. Or touch her shoulder. Or take her hand.

He didn't.

"I don't blame you," she said.

"What?"

"For this. For all of this. It's not your fault. He could have gotten lost in the city just as easily. More easily. It's not your fault."

He understood the words: they were clear enough. But in her broken voice, they seemed to mean the opposite of what she was saying. All he heard was Diane blaming him. And it was true. This was his fault. This never would have happened in the city. Never would have happened if his mother had been taking care of him.

He bit the inside of his lip until it bled.

"Did they . . . do they have any . . ."

He had to take a deep breath before he could speak. "Jim said there are lots of trails, some of them really new. They can't tell if they're from today, but they're really recent."

As the crew had returned to the yard, Jim Kelly, one of the owners of the Henderson Press, had been shaking his head and rubbing his hands together. "Jesus, it's cold out there."

He stopped himself, seeing the look on Jeff's face. "Sorry," he said, sheepishly.

"That's all right." It was cold; it wasn't like he hadn't noticed.

"I'm gonna pop back into the office, grab my good gloves." And a drink, Jeff assumed. "Is there anything you want from town?"

Jeff had shaken his head, and Jim had wandered up the driveway toward his truck.

"Do you want to come downstairs?" he asked Diane, both of them watching the Search and Rescue crew girding themselves with reflective vests, and helmets with lights. "Claire's made some sandwiches."

"I'll stay here," she said, her voice dead.

"All right," he said, and waited, but she said nothing more, and a moment later he turned away.

Carly was waiting for Brian when he got to their meeting place early the next morning. She smiled when she saw him.

"You came," she said.

He nodded, trying not to show how thrilled he was to see her. "Sorry if I made you wait."

"No, I don't mind. I was just hoping you hadn't forgotten about me."

The thought shocked Brian. It had never occurred to him that she might be looking forward to seeing him as much as he had been looking forward to seeing her.

"I made some sandwiches," he said, tugging off his backpack. "Did you want one? Peanut butter and jam."

She shook her head. "No, thank you." She patted the log next to her. "Why don't you sit here while you eat?"

He was shaking a little as he sat down next to her. When he tried to unwrap his sandwiches, even his hands were shaking.

He hoped she wouldn't notice.

The day passed in what felt to Brian like mere moments. They wandered trails he had never seen, pointed things out to one another they hadn't previously noticed. Carly showed him a thrush nest, high in a tree, and Brian climbed the tree and showed her how the feathers connected to their shafts under his microscope. They talked and laughed and walked in easy silence, holding hands.

It was an endless series of perfect moments.

As the shadows thickened, she stopped him and held both of his hands. "You have to go?" she asked.

It hadn't even occurred to him to look at the time: it was already almost 4:30. "I can stay a little longer," he said, thinking of the way his father hadn't even noticed he was gone the day before. Then he corrected himself. "No, no. I should go. If I'm late my dad might not let me come out after school tomorrow."

The look of sadness that had crossed her face lifted, broke into a smile. "You'll come back?" she asked, as if she couldn't believe her ears.

"Of course I will," he said.

She squeezed his hands, leaned in quickly and kissed his cheek, turning away immediately, as if embarrassed.

His face started to warm.

"Here," she said, dropping one of his hands to sweep aside a dense, hanging branch. Stepping through, Brian found himself back in the clearing at the edge of the forest.

"Tomorrow?" she asked again.

He smiled, "Tomorrow."

She squeezed his hand.

The hours seemed to crawl by, with nothing for Jeff to do but wait. He wandered through the yard, slowly, keeping one eye on the dark smudge of forest, alert to the occasional flash of lights from its edge. His heart jumped every time someone came out, every time there was a crackle from Charlie's radio truck, thinking that maybe this was when it would happen, maybe this was when Brian would come back.

There were people everywhere, the driveway so full of cars that anyone arriving had to park on the shoulder of the road and walk in, but he felt completely alone.

Around midnight, when he noticed Jeff pacing up the driveway, Dean Owens disengaged himself from the group he was talking with and met him halfway. Dean was wearing a heavy coat with a reflective vest over top. The sight of him, and his misty breath in the night air, made Jeff think of Brian in the woods, in the dark, scared, shivering—

He tried to block out the image.

"Any news?" he asked Dean.

"Not what you're wanting to hear. The teams met mid-point in the woods about an hour ago. There's no sign of your son."

Jeff flinched despite himself.

Dean shook his head. "That's not necessarily a bad thing. If he'd been swept into one of the creeks or attacked by an animal, we would have found something. His pack, maybe." He paused, shook his head and touched Jeff's shoulder. "I'm tellin' you this straight, because you're a friend: the fact that we haven't found his pack or anything is a good sign. It means he's holding onto it. It means he's probably all together. See what I'm telling you?"

Jeff nodded, barely able to conceal his sudden need to vomit.

The true magnitude of the situation washed over him like a chilling storm. He had spent that evening downplaying everything in his mind, expecting the Search and Rescue to find Brian easily, if he wasn't going to walk out of the woods on his own.

But neither of those things had happened. And now he couldn't shake the image of his son floating down one of the swollen creeks, his backpack soaked and heavy, keeping him just under the surface.

"What—" His voice came out broken and soft. Jeff coughed to clear his throat. "What do we do next?"

Dean took a deep breath. "We've split up the team that

started from this side. They're going to move out from your fence lines through John and Claire's place that way, and over young Tom's place that way. The team that started at the logging road is going back in, but in the other direction. Toward the mountain."

"But he's not—he knows to keep to this side of the logging road. He wouldn't—"

Dean smiled and shook his head. "I seem to recall you and me taking a few liberties with *your* father's rules, too. Right?"

Jeff hesitated, then nodded.

"You remember what it's like when you get out there. A lot of the rules don't seem to apply so much. Doesn't make him a bad kid. Just a kid."

"Right." Jeff nodded again. "But"—he glanced at his watch—"it's almost one in the morning. When do you—"

"Call off the search for the night?"

"Yeah."

"We don't. If this was an alpine search, we probably would have called it off at sundown. Mountain terrain is too treacherous to mess around with after dark. But this is pretty flat, pretty straightforward. We can search through the night if we need to."

"That's good."

Dean nodded. "The crews have been spelling off for the last while. Fresh eyes so the first crew can get some rest."

"What about you?"

"John Sears came on about an hour ago. I was just waiting to let you know what was going on."

Jeff felt suddenly as if he wanted to cry: the small kindness was overwhelming. "Thanks, Dean," he said.

Dean shook his head and clapped him on the shoulder. "You should get inside. Your wife'll be starting to worry about you."

Ex-wife, Jeff was about to say, but Dean had already turned away.

By the time the school bus brought him home and he had changed into his scrubbies from his good clothes, Brian had little more than an hour with Carly. Spring might have come early, but night still came on fast. Too fast. Especially on school nights.

They made the most of their time together. Carly was always waiting for him, and every day brought new wonders. Baby animals were being born everywhere—a blue jay's nest one day, a rabbit den another—and the forest itself was changing, greening and thickening. The creeks were rising with the spring run-off, and the swamps burst into sudden colour: yellows and purples and oranges of flowers half-hidden in the shadows.

And everyday it was harder to say goodbye. When it came time, Brian would leave it as long as he could, reluctant to let go of her, of their time together, even as the house started to disappear in the falling dark.

He took solace in the knowledge that there was always

tomorrow, that he would be back in the woods with her in only a matter of hours.

But then the rains came, black sheets of March rain that soaked one to the bone in an instant, that chilled one to the core.

It rained for days, the creeks rising and rising and almost slipping their beds, the animals slinking through the low brush only when absolutely necessary, and all Brian could do was look out at the woods as the rain streaked his bedroom window.

Carly was waiting for him in their usual spot three days later. From the bulging grey look of the sky the rains hadn't finished, but they had stopped for the moment, and Brian had hurried across the field as soon as he got changed from school.

"Carly," he called as he stepped under the forest's canopy, stopping short as he saw her.

A tight frown was fixed on her face.

"You didn't come," she said, not meeting his eyes.

"I'm sorry."

"You said you'd come every day."

"It was raining," he said, as if that was reason enough.

"I waited for you." She finally looked up at him, long enough for him to see the hurt in her eyes, then back down to the ground again.

"I'm sorry," he repeated. "My dad . . ." His father hadn't actually said anything about it: it hadn't even occurred to Brian to spend the dark, rainy afternoons in the forest. He hadn't thought for a moment she would be there.

At the mention of his father, she looked up again, and her eyes seemed a little clearer, more understanding. "I *waited*," she said again, but sounding sad this time, not angry.

"I'm sorry. I'm here now."

Her smile broke through her frown and he felt a weight lift from him. "You are. You came back." All around them, the leaves and boughs dripped as if the rain was still coming down. "Come on." She started toward the forest.

"Wait."

She stopped.

"Are you—" He gestured toward her. "You don't have a coat or anything." He had bundled himself into a slicker over his jacket but already felt the damp and the cold; she wore the same dress as always, her face pink and rosy.

She smiled at his concern. "I'll be fine," she said. "I love the rain."

As they walked he tried, as he always did, to impose their route on his mental map of the forest he thought he had come to know. They walked past the reading place— the lightning-struck tree with the cave in its trunk where he used to sit and read his guidebook—and the broken-down section of fence grown over with blackberries, the young canes thin and bright green. They crossed one of the creeks, the water rough and almost covering the tops of the stepping stones.

By Brian's reckoning, the next turn should have brought them to a clearing full of huckleberries and salmonberries that would be ripe in the early summer.

Instead, she led him into a bright grove, rich with a

heady blur of unfamiliar scents. The sky was bright blue and warm overhead. *The storm must have burned off while they were under the trees*, Brian thought, suddenly too warm in his heavy coat.

"What is this place?" he asked, mostly to himself.

Carly smiled, looking pleased with herself. "I thought you'd like it."

Brian stepped into the clearing, brushed his hands along the trunk of one of the flowering trees. "I don't think I've ever seen this plant."

"It's a magnolia."

"Do they usually grow around here?" He wanted to open his knapsack, pull out his guidebook, but he couldn't look away from the grove. The clearing had the sharp brilliance, the bright detail, of a dream, and Brian was sure it would vanish if he looked away.

"And those are cypresses," Carly said, leading him farther in. "Touch them. They feel warm. And their bark—"

"—feels like skin," he finished, lightly caressing the smooth, red-brown trunk.

He didn't want to look away, but he turned to Carly. "How . . . where are we? I've never—"

She smiled, as if she had a secret. "We're in the forest," she explained. "Your house is just over there." She gestured vaguely.

"But . . . how can that be? There's nothing like this in the woods. How far have we gone?"

"It's not how far you go," she said. "It's how you look. All of this, these trees, these flowers, this place, it's all here. It's *all* right here. All forests are one forest, if you know how to look at them."

He knew she wanted him to ask. And he wanted to ask. He wanted to know.

"Could you— Could you show me?"

She seemed to think about it, then slowly shook her head. "No. Not now. We don't have enough time."

"Sure we do," he countered. The sun was still high in the sky, bright and warm. "It's only—" He was stunned when he looked at his watch and saw that it was already after five. "But . . . how . . ."

"You have to go home, Brian," she said, taking his arm and turning him away from the clearing. "It's time."

They stepped through a scrim of low brambles and twisted weeds and the air chilled around them.

"We just don't have enough time," she said. "Not for me to show you everything I want to show you. Not for you to see everything you want to see. I probably shouldn't even have taken you there."

"No," he said, his words coming in puffs of steam. "No, I'm glad you did. Maybe tomorrow you can show me more."

"Maybe," she said, as they stepped into the overhung clearing at the edge of the forest. "Maybe tomorrow."

Her voice didn't sound very convincing.

"You will be here tomorrow, right?" Brian asked.

"I'll be here," she said. "You should go."

He didn't want to leave her. A feeling that had been building in him for several days bubbled to the surface. He began to feel that his time with Carly was short, coming to an end. Every time he said goodbye to her, it felt like he was saying goodbye for the last time.

He didn't want to leave. He didn't want to risk not seeing her again.

"Your father will be wondering where you've got to," she said.

"You'll be here tomorrow?" he asked again, needing, with a part of himself he didn't understand, to hear it confirmed.

She nodded, and the warmth of her confirmation ebbed through him. "I'll be here."

He smiled, and turned slowly away.

She watched him as he crossed the field, pulling his jacket tight and hunching his back against the rain. She felt his yearning in his defeated stride, his wanting to stay as an invisible line, binding them.

She smiled, and faded back into the gathering shadows.

Jeff wasn't surprised to find John Joseph in his kitchen, though he was somewhat surprised to find him washing dishes.

"Thought I'd get a head start," he explained. "Lots of coffee cups. Did you talk with Dean Owens? He said he was going to wait for you."

Jeff nodded, not really aware that he was doing so. He felt himself moving as if within a bubble, distant somehow from the events of his own life.

John watched him for a moment, then dried his hands and led him toward the kitchen table. "Why don't you set a minute," he said. "Take a load off. I'll get you a little something."

"Diane?" Jeff asked as John rattled in the kitchen cupboards.

"Last I checked she was up in your boy's room," John said. "It seemed like she wanted to be alone. Oh, and Jim Kelly left that for you," he added as he returned to the table, moving a folded piece of paper toward Jeff as he set a bottle of rye and two glasses down. "He said he thought you might get a kick out of it. Seemed like he'd been into the rye a bit himself."

Jeff nodded again, his gaze resting on the bottle. He watched it as John unscrewed the top, poured healthy measures into both glasses. He left the metal cap sitting on the table next to the bottle when he set it down.

"This'll help take the chill off." John pushed one of the glasses toward Jeff.

Jeff took a small sip, then a larger swallow, staring into the amber liquid in the glass as the sweetness burned down his throat.

It seemed to cut through some of the fog.

He unfolded the paper, keenly aware of John Joseph looking over his shoulder.

"What . . ."

It was a photocopy of the front page of the March 21, 1975 issue of the Henderson Herald. The banner headline read: "Lost and Found," with a large black and white photograph underneath. Jeff recognized himself with a shocked immediacy, though he had to read the caption for the names of the men he was standing between.

"Donald TeBrink and Charles Ellroy with Jeffrey Page, who was missing in his family's woods for more than twenty-four hours."

John gave a short chuckle and wandered back to the sink.

Jeff skimmed the article, but his eyes kept drifting back to the photo. He wouldn't have recognized Charlie without the write-up: the "Charles" in the photograph had all of his hair, and was wearing it more than a little long, with an open collar and a beaded necklace. He had a broad grin that showed just how pleased he was that someone wanted to take his picture for the paper.

His own expression was harder to read. At first, his eleven-year-old face seemed a little scared and a little relieved, as you might expect from a little boy rescued from the woods. Looking at it again, though—studying it—Jeff wasn't so sure. He thought his eleven-year-old self looked almost sad. Not scared, but close to tears.

As he shifted the paper, hoping a different angle would help him puzzle out his expression, Jeff noticed, for the first time, the faces crowded around behind the three figures in the foreground. The rest of the searchers, he assumed, milling around, only half-interested in the photographer, not meriting, for whatever reason, having their names on the front page of the local paper.

Most of them were out of focus, but one face, just over his younger self's right shoulder, was instantly recognizable.

John Joseph wasn't looking toward the camera, but the lens had found him nonetheless.

When he looked up, John Joseph was staring at him, holding his own glass close to his lips.

"But I don't . . . I don't remember. I don't remember any of it. I look at this"—he tapped on the photocopied page—"and I know it's true, but I don't remember. . . ." He barked out a sharp, desperate laugh. "'Least you could have done was tell me you were part of the crew that rescued me."

John chuckled. "I seem the type to hide my light under a bushel to you?" He shook his head. "No, I'd have taken the credit if there was any to be taken."

"What do you mean?" Jeff asked, pulling the paper toward himself again and taking another look.

"I mean that nobody rescued you, Jeff." He drained his glass, lowering his eyelids as he swallowed. "We spent a full day and night out back there. We must have covered every inch of your father's woods. And mine. And old Tom's. Crews even started up the hill, thinking you might have decided to try your hand at mountain climbing."

He stopped to pour himself another couple of fingers of rye, and topped up Jeff's drink.

"Then just before sunset the second day, you walked out of the woods."

"I just . . . ?"

John nodded. "All of your own accord, and under your own steam. You were cold and hungry." The old man smiled. "You looked like a boy who had been out in the woods for a night and a day."

Jeff smiled ruefully, staring down at his glass. He felt something that seemed like it might be a memory niggling at the edges of his mind, but nothing came into focus.

"And you were crying."

The words hung in the air as if placed there.

Jeff looked across the table at the old man.

"Crying?"

He nodded. "Sobbing. Everyone thought it was because you had been so scared, that you were so relieved at being home. Everybody comforted you, told you it was going to be all right."

"But?"

John pushed himself away from the table, carried his empty glass to the sink and gave it a rinse. He leaned against the counter, looking to the window over the sink, the window that during the day offered a view of the woods. He spoke to the reflection of Jeff in the night dark glass.

"Adults don't always listen to children," he said, quietly. "We think we know exactly who they are, exactly what they need, exactly what they're going to say."

Jeff stiffened in the chair.

"We think we know what they're feeling, and we just proceed along with our assumptions. If we ever took the time to actually listen . . ."

"I get it," Jeff said, not angrily. "I should have paid more attention to Brian. I should have really listened to what he was trying to tell me about not moving to Vancouver."

John turned away from the glass to face him directly.

"That sounds about right, but I don't have any idea what you're talking about."

"Then what . . ."

"They should have listened to *you* better, that day you came out of the woods. Everyone was so busy bringing you blankets and food and telling you that everything was going to be all right, no one actually heard what you were crying about. No one listened to what you were saying."

"Nobody except you," Jeff said, his voice a hoarse whisper.

John nodded slowly. "You kept saying, 'She's gone. She's gone and I'm never going to see her again. Carly's gone.'"

———————————

"You're late," were his father's first words as the screen door clattered shut behind Brian.

"Sorry, Dad," he called up the stairs as he kicked off his shoes and hung up his jacket and slicker.

He couldn't stop smiling.

The apology, he thought, *would be enough.* His dad didn't usually get mad. And even less now, with his mom gone and living in Vancouver. Since she left, Brian had noticed that his father seemed to be working very hard at not getting mad, at not raising his voice, at not doing anything to upset Brian.

The apology would probably be enough.

It wasn't.

He came around the corner at the top of the stairs, holding a spatula in his hand. "Where were you?" he demanded.

Brian couldn't tell if he was really angry or just worried, but looking up at him from the bottom of the stairs, he felt tiny.

"Out in the woods," he answered, in a voice as small as he felt.

"What are the rules?"

"Home before dark. Home before dinner."

"Right."

Brian started to climb the stairs. Every step felt like an obstacle, seemed to take all his focus.

"Sorry, Dad."

"That's not good enough, Brian."

As he reached the top of the stairs, his father turned away from him and went back to the stove. The kitchen was full of the smell of toasting bread and frying butter: grilled cheese sandwiches and tomato soup for dinner.

"You've been getting later and later everyday. It's almost six," he said, without facing his son. "I didn't make up these rules to be a pain in the ass. I need to know where you are. I need to know that you're safe. And every day you're pushing these boundaries more and more."

"Dad, I'm—"

"Jesus, Brian, it's pitch dark out there. I thought I was going to have to call out the Search and Rescue."

"We just—" As soon as the words were out of his mouth, he realized the slip. He wanted desperately to call the words back, to undo the damage he had done. For a moment, he hoped his father hadn't heard.

His father turned to him. "We?"

"Why don't you come home with me?" he had asked Carly during one of their first afternoons together.

She had shaken her head.

"Why not? I'm sure my dad wouldn't mind."

"I think we should keep all this just between us," she had said. "I don't think you should tell your father anything about me. It can be our little secret."

"All right," he said, a little hesitantly, not really understanding. "But why—"

"He just wouldn't understand."

"Who's we?"

How much to say? How much to reveal?

"Just Carly." He went to the cupboard and brought down two plates and two bowls and started setting the table.

"Who's Carly? Is she someone from school?"

"No, I think she lives on one of the big farms. She dresses like the girls who go to that other school."

It was a good answer: his father seemed to relax a little bit. He turned back to the stove, stirred the pot of soup.

"Is she out there all the time with you?"

He knew instinctively not to let his guard down. "Most days, I guess." He knew better than to tell his father about how she was always waiting for him, or about the places she had shown him. Or about what had happened that afternoon.

His father nodded slowly. "Okay," he said. "I wish you

had mentioned her sooner."

Brian paused in the cutlery drawer. "Why?"

He sighed and turned off the stove. "It might have . . . Your mom and I, we worry about you. I know how much you like it back there, and I know how much you like being alone, but it makes me feel better to know you're not always on your own."

Brian allowed himself to relax. It felt like a storm has passed, that he had wiggled his way out from his father's anger. As he set the cutlery by the plates, he felt his smile returning. He tried to contain it, but couldn't. The feelings were just too big.

She had kissed him.

That was why he had been late.

They had been saying goodbye at the forest's edge when she had leaned in and brushed her lips against his. Her lips had been dry, and when she stepped back she had looked away, down at her feet.

"*What—*" *He couldn't even put the question together, his mind speeding in small concentric circles, his heart vibrating wildly in his chest.*

"*I'm sorry,*" *she said softly, still looking at the ground. "I didn't mean to . . ."*

"*No,*" *he stopped her. "No, I . . ."*

"*It's just that—*" *She looked up at him, her head still angled toward the ground, her eyes almost hidden by the fall of her hair. "It's just—*"

"*It's okay.*" *His face was hot.*

"*I just like you. An awful lot. And I hate it when you have to go. I miss you." Her words came in whispered bursts, as if she had to steel herself for every phrase.*

"You . . . like me?"

She had nodded, looking up at him slowly, shyly.

His father was staring at him strangely from across the table, and Brian felt the stretch of his smile pulling at the corners of his mouth.

"Good soup, Dad," he said, trying to draw his attention away.

They sat side by side on the fallen log. Brian was keenly aware of how close she was to him, how near her hand, resting on her leg, was to his own.

"It's hard for me when you have to go," she said, looking toward the scrim of undergrowth that separated the worlds of forests and fields. "I miss you."

"I miss you, too." Until that moment, he wouldn't have really been able to label his feelings. He hadn't realized that his thinking of her, his wanting to be with her, the empty space within himself when he was away from her, had a name.

He knew about missing someone, of course. Since his mother had gone, he had missed her every day. But this was different. Stronger. Sharper.

"I don't like having to leave."

She turned to look at him, her eyes the pale green of a spring leaf. Without thinking, he reached out and took her hand, entwining his fingers through hers. Looking into her eyes, he was surprised to see her need there. He had thought, until that moment, that he was the only one who felt the absence of someone so deeply, that he was alone in missing someone so much it physically ached.

"I talked to your mom on the phone today," his father said, scraping his spoon along the bottom of his mostly empty bowl. "We talked a long time."

Something in his father's voice made Brian look up. "About what?"

"About you," his father said, setting the spoon down. "About the fall."

"What about the fall?"

"Your mom . . . your mom and I, like I said, we're a bit worried. About you. About how much time you're spending on your own. We think . . . we think it might be best if you tried going to school in the city next year."

"No!" he cried out sharply, before he knew he was doing it.

His father nodded. "I know this is a bit of a surprise, but we've been talking about it."

"You never talked to me."

"There's a lot of programs you can do after school, a lot of opportunities that Henderson just doesn't have."

"But . . ."

"And it's not right away. You'll finish up this year here, and we'll get you moved over the summer. I figure you can come home every weekend if you want."

"What if I don't want to go at all?"

"Brian, it's—"

"What if I want to stay here?"

"Your mom and I—"

"I don't want to go!"

His father sighed. "Let's not get into a fight about this, all right? When you're there next week, I think you'll see—"

"Next week?"

"Spring break," his father explained. "You're spending the week with your mom. She thought it might be a good chance . . ."

"Next week?"

"We've talked about this."

"Right." He vaguely remembered them talking about it, looking at the calendar, how excited his mom had been about it during the last weekend at her apartment in the city.

But that had all been before he met Carly.

The thought of her tightened his stomach into a hard ball.

"When is she coming to pick me up?" he asked.

"Sunday afternoon. And she said she'd bring you back around dinnertime the next Sunday, so you'll have a full week."

Brian nodded and looked down at his bowl, unable to even think of having another bite.

"I know it's a lot, Brian. But I think—"

"Can I be excused?"

His father seemed to deflate. "Yeah. Clear your dishes."

For a moment, just before Brian turned away, a look of sadness flashed across his father's face, an expression he tried to hide.

He doesn't want me to go. He thinks I don't want to go because I'll miss him.

The thought cut through Brian, forcing him to look again at his father, to see the deep sadness just under his skin, the dark behind his eyes.

He didn't like seeing that sadness, that weakness, in his father. He didn't like knowing that he had done something to put it there, that the mere thought of his absence was enough to hurt him.

Missing him.

He didn't like admitting to himself that he hadn't even considered his father when he thought of having to move to the city.

All he had thought about was Carly.

Missing her.

The lights were still off in Brian's room. Jeff could hardly see Diane in the spill of the work lights through the curtains. She was curled on her side on Brian's bed, her knees pulled in tight to her chest. She faced away from the door, toward the window.

Her breathing was deep and regular.

Jeff crept into the room, silent, trying not to disturb her.

He stood behind the bed. Through the window he could see the wall of the shop, the slow, gentle spread of the field, and the wall of darkness that was the forest behind.

He sat down carefully at the foot of the bed.

There is no lonelier sound than the deep, calm, in and out of another's breath beside you, nothing that can make you feel quite so distant, quite so removed.

He had once taken comfort in Diane's breathing next to him, the calm regularity of it providing solace and reassurance in the darkest hours of the night.

When had that changed? When had that sound started to make him feel so crushingly alone?

"He's not coming back, is he?" she asked quietly, in a voice that was strong and clear but still bore the echo of tears.

The sound startled him. "I thought you were asleep."

"No."

The silence, the space between them, was deep and wide. He wanted to cross it, to reach out to touch her, but he no longer knew her. And he couldn't bear to have her pull away from him.

"I've been lying here, listening to them outside. I hear their voices, but I can't make out what they're saying. They're not going to find him."

"Don't say that."

In another time, she would have rolled on her back, or to face him. They would have looked into one another's eyes, found a way to comfort each other.

But she remained on her side, facing away.

"They'll find him," Jeff said, but as he spoke, he realized that he didn't believe the words himself.

The sun was bright and warm, but the air was cool and smelled of the sea. Was Brian imagining it, or did he hear the faint sound of waves in the distance?

He followed Carly down the steep slope, his pack bouncing occasionally off moss-covered rocks and damp tree trunks. He kept one eye on the terrain around him and one eye on Carly. She was a fair ways ahead, moving over the rough ground with a light ease and grace, a natural comfort Brian envied. This was her world: she fit into it as naturally as the birdsong in the air, as the spongy, mossy ground under his feet.

Could he ever be as comfortable here? Would he get to a point where he could seem to float between obstacles, to step gracefully between worlds?

Every so often she would stop and look back at him, smiling broadly, encouragingly. There was no impatience, no sense that he was holding her back or that she was waiting for him. Looking at her, someone would think she had all the time in the world.

"We're almost there," she called.

"Where?" he called back, steadying himself with a thin tree trunk.

"You'll see."

He thought these were the most wonderful words someone had ever said to him, and Carly said them all the time. *You'll see.* Spending time with her was a world of surprises through every copse of trees, through every stand of brush, in every clearing. It was a world of wonders that she revealed to him in every moment.

And she herself was one of those wonders.

You'll see.

She was waiting for him in a small clearing. The sound of waves was louder here, the smell of salt and spray sharp and intoxicating.

She looked at him coyly, but didn't say anything.

He stepped toward her slowly.

"Look," she said, stepping to one side to reveal the most beautiful plant he had ever seen.

It was pure white, shimmering and almost translucent, so bright it almost hurt his eyes. It had no leaves, only a thick white stem and a number of small white flowers. I was clearly a plant, but just barely.

It looked like something out of a dream.

Brian stepped forward, crouched in the loamy softness as he bent to examine the plant.

"What is this?" He leaned in close to study the texture of the stem, the flower, afraid to touch it.

"It has a lot of different names," she said, leaning in with him. "Some people call it the coast orchid, or the albino orchid." Her voice was a whisper. "I call it the death rose."

"Why?"

"Because it lives off the dead." When he looked at her, she was looking at the plant, but he knew she had been looking at him a moment before. "It has no leaves because it never sees the sun. It grows in the shadows, and takes its strength from the rot and decay of the earth around it. It grows from the dead."

"Like a fungus," he whispered.

"Sort of."

Without looking away from the plant, Brian pulled off his pack and unzipped it.

"It won't be in your guide," she said, just as he curled his fingers around the book's spine to pull it out.

"Why not?"

"To most of the world, the death rose doesn't exist. It grows in only three places, three of these tiny valleys just off the coast where it can drink the moisture out of the air, where it can consume the past through its roots."

"But people must know about it."

She nodded. "People do. But those few who have seen it know they have been in the presence of something extraordinary, something profound. Something that transcends classification. Something that just *is*."

She looked at him as she spoke.

He released his grip on the book and let the bag fall to the cool, damp earth.

She smiled.

"Probably no more than a hundred people have seen this flower in the last century," she said.

"It's amazing."

"There are others," she started, and he looked at her. "Other secret places like this. Plants and animals you won't find in any book. Places you won't find on any map."

Their eyes met, and he didn't look away.

"There's a flower, an African orchid, that only blooms one night every seven years. It is believed that if you pick this flower and give it to your heart's true love before the sun rises, it will never die, and your love will be the stuff of legends."

Her eyes stayed on his, rich and green and bottomless.

"And there's a forest of trees so tall"—she stopped, as if she couldn't believe it herself—"that they make the tallest trees near your house seem like twigs."

He watched her mouth as she formed the words, her eyes as she seemed to drift into the stories she told.

"You could spend a lifetime—many lifetimes—discovering the wonders of this world all around you."

Yes, he admitted to himself, at last. *I could.*

Joe Phelps manned the Communications Centre in the Search and Rescue truck. The crackling of radio signals and distant voices were the only sounds in the still yard, just touched with the first light of dawn.

Jeff set the mug he was carrying on the desktop beside Joe. "I thought you could use this."

Joe tugged off the headphones he was wearing. "Thanks, Jeff," he said, and he looked like he was about to say something else but turned away, directing his attention back to his switches and knobs.

It took Jeff a moment. "It's all right, Joe. I'm not out

here trying to get information from you or anything. I know you'll let us know if there's any news."

The relief on Joe's face was palpable.

"I just thought you might like some coffee. It's been a long night." He stepped back, took a sip from his own mug. The sun was starting to rise and the world was grey, a mist clinging to the lows of the field.

Joe seemed almost chagrined. "Yeah. Thanks for . . . for the coffee."

Jeff shook his head as if to dismiss it. "I was coming out anyhow. I'm gonna . . . I'm just gonna take a walk up—" He couldn't bring himself to say the words. "Just up to the edge."

"Sure." Jeff turned away, then back as Joe added, "We'll let you know. As soon as we know something. We'll find him."

Jeff looked at him for a long moment, then turned away, without speaking.

He walked only to the grassy verge edging the west field. He could have walked straight up the drive, past the shop and the old barn and behind it, where the track ended at the forest's edge. It was the most direct route.

But that didn't feel right. Something drove him away from the yard, through the field to the edge of the wood.

Was it the picture of himself? Some memory he couldn't consciously grasp?

For whatever reason, he was sure this was the path that Brian had taken, that he was following in his son's footsteps.

The way his son had been following in his.

Like father, like son.

As the sun crested over the mountains, the dew on the grass shone silver, a wet, shining carpet leading inexorably into the darkness.

He stopped at the point where the grass met the brown of the forest floor. Under the spread of the trees, the light disappeared, and the night still felt almost full.

He had to steel himself to step across the dividing line into the forest.

Once under the trees, it took Jeff's eyes a moment to adjust, vague shapes gradually shifting and congealing into forms: stumps and bushes, a fallen log, a stand of trilliums. The clearing was familiar.

As was the girl who stepped soundlessly into the clearing from the dense brush.

"Carly?" he whispered, as if afraid she might take flight.

She smiled. "I didn't think you'd remember."

"I didn't," he said.

But now he did.

Without warning, he remembered it all.

The weight of the fishing rod on his shoulder, the tackle box in his pack. The smell of the forest, fresh and green, in his nose, his clothes, his skin. The taste of the trout he had caught with her in the tumble-rocked mountain stream, its sweetness, and the bracing cold of the water they had drunk. The feel of her hand in his. The stars so bright in the sky the night they had spent in the woods, the Northern Lights dancing above them.

He had never seen the Northern Lights again.

And he remembered crying, feeling something rent from him, a tugging at his heart that left him gasping for breath.

He remembered her asking—

"I asked if you wanted to stay with me," she said.

Did she sound sad, even a little? Jeff thought so.

"I remember."

"You said you had to go home."

"I'm sorry."

She shook her head. "I understand. I understood, even then. You wanted to stay. I could tell. I wouldn't have asked otherwise. But you had to go home."

He didn't say anything, remembering the sound of her voice. He hadn't heard it in more than thirty years, but it was so familiar to him he was amazed he could have forgotten.

"I wanted to stay," he said, lost in the memories of his time with her. She had shown him worlds he could only imagine, worlds he had lost when he stepped away from her.

"I know."

"Is . . . Is Brian with you?" The words came hard, and he already knew the answer.

"Yes."

Jeff felt an unaccountable relief. Brian wasn't lost. Brian was just . . . gone.

"Did you ask him to stay with you?" His voice broke on the whispered words.

She looked at him.

"No," she said.

His heart clutched at a final hope.

"He asked me."

A sob rose in his throat, but he pushed it back down.

He remembered the places she had taken them. The air was so pure, the light so bright, everything outlined with a subtle glow.

And he knew he had spent the years since he had turned away from her, spent his whole life, in a world of greys and half-measures, the reality around him a pale shadow of the worlds he had tasted. The worlds he had lost.

"Is . . . is he safe?"

When she smiled, the clearing seemed to glow around them. "He's blessed."

The words caught at his breath and tore it away. "Be . . . Take good care of him," he said, in a voice hollow and powerless.

"He'll come to no harm with me," she said, and though the words were soothing, they did not take away his pain.

When she stepped away, turned back to the forest and faded into the green and brown, Jeff Page fell to his knees, his back heaving with broken sobs as he cried for what was lost. For what he knew would not return.

After breakfast the Sunday morning he disappeared, Brian had gone up to his room. The sound of the back door closing as his father went out to his shop echoed through the house.

He had barely slept the night before, too filled with excitement, with thoughts of the day—the days—ahead.

He unzipped his knapsack and set it on his bed for filling. The microscope in its case took up most of the space. He slid the plant guide in beside it, and a sweater. He didn't think he'd need clothes, but he was a bit worried that he might be cold at night.

Looking around the room, he tried to figure out what else he might need. His compass. A magnifying glass. The picture of the three of them—he and his mother and his father all together—that had been taken at Disneyland. The slingshot his father had given him.

The thought of his father made Brian pause. He wasn't mad at his father. Carly was right: he just didn't understand.

He thought of leaving him a note, but he had no idea what he would write. He knew his father and mother would be sad or scared, but there were no words to explain what he was doing, where he was going, what it all meant.

As he zipped up his backpack, he took a last look around his room. The books on his shelves. The posters on his walls. The schoolbooks on his desk.

As he walked down the stairs, he trailed his fingers along the cool walls, listened to the echo of his footsteps.

He took one last look around the kitchen, at the table where he and his father ate every meal, at the dishes on the counter, at the toast on his plate.

He slipped on his boots and coat, and closed the back door for the last time.

He stopped in front of the open door to the shop, and looked inside. The smell of oil tickled his nose, the way it always did. His father was under the car, his sticking-out legs the only part of him that was visible.

He didn't speak. Tears streaming down his face, he raised his hand in farewell, and turned away, setting out across the field for the woods.

Jeff Page never told anyone what had happened to him in the woods, either as a boy or that morning after Brian disappeared.

The search for the missing boy went on for weeks. Newspapers as far away as Toronto wrote about the disappearance, and TV crews from the city parked their vans in the field beside the house. Diane answered most of their questions. When they had Jeff on-camera, he was barely able to articulate his loss. He seemed to have given up, long before the searchers did.

Some days, after the search, after the headlines, Jeff would find himself in the woods with no awareness of how he had got there. He would find the quiet of a clearing near the forest's edge, or tuck himself into the lightning-struck cave at the base of a giant cedar tree, and just sit. He would sit for hours without moving, listening to the wind in the leaves, the sound of birds around him.

He would sit for hours, waiting, hoping to hear, just

once, the echo of distant laughter.

And at night, he would stand in the dew-wet grass of the back lawn as the dusk settled around him, looking out at the darkening swath of trees, the black hill behind them. He would stand there until full dark, looking for small, luminous figures in the distance, waiting to hear his son call to him, Brian's reedy voice calling to invite him to come away with them.

He would have gone.

But the call never came.

And once the full dark came on, he would turn away, walk back into the house. He would close the door behind him, but not lock it.

He never locked the door again.

And he always left a light burning.

NOTES

I wrote this novella over the course of a month or so in the summer of 2006, using a Lamy 2000 fountain pen loaded with Noodlers Black in a standard issue, middle-grade composition notebook.

While I was writing, I was listening, exclusively, to the first two albums by The Band: *Music From Big Pink* and *The Band*. Something about those songs, utterly contemporary (even now, some forty years after their release), yet utterly timeless, put me in the perfect mindset for this story, set as it is on the rubicon between contemporary and traditional storytelling, between domestic reality and mythic fantasy. At one point, I decided to change the music—a month is a long time to spend several hours every morning listening to the same two records, over and over—and almost immediately, the writing stopped. So, after a day or two of frustration, I put the albums back on. It seemed to do the trick.

This story was finished sitting in the woods a short distance away from the shores of Cowichan Lake, smoking a cigar and listening to my son in the distance, playing in the water with his aunt and uncle, his mother and grandmother. It was one of those perfect moments.

The title of this novella is lifted shamelessly from "The Stolen Child" by W.B. Yeats. The poem was an inspiration, but it's not an answer, should you be inclined to look for one.

PLACES
&
NAMES

Mom, this one's for you. And for anyone reading in
Agassiz, BC ("The Corn Capital of British Columbia").
And for anyone else who might be wondering.

ome truths are slow to sink in; there are things that you know, implicitly, without necessarily grasping their full implications. Over the last year, for example, it has been brought vividly to my awareness that, despite the best of intentions, writers often don't know just what they're writing, even as they're writing it.

I should have known, though. That fact was certainly brought home to me a few years ago, when my first novel, *Before I Wake*, hit the shelves and people started asking me questions that simply hadn't occurred to me. I realized then, from their questions, that there were whole aspects of that book that I had no real awareness of having explored.

If you were to ask, I would tell you that—consciously—I'm a narrative-focused writer. To my mind, story is the main thing. Give me a good plot, and some good characters to see it through, and that's all I can ask for. I don't get hung up on the language of a story or novel; in fact, I prefer that the language be as transparent as possible, not drawing attention to itself and, more importantly, not drawing attention away from the story and the characters.

When people started asking me about Before I Wake, though, I realized that I also wrote—completely unbeknownst to myself—with a considerable emphasis on the novel's sense of place. To such a point that people, especially readers in Victoria, were singling out that aspect of the book for special emphasis.

And there was always one question that came up, over and over again: why Victoria? Why had I chosen to set the novel in Victoria?

The answer I tended to give might have seemed flip to those asking the question, but it wasn't, really. It was the only answer I could honestly give: I set *Before I Wake* in Victoria because that's where it happened.

No, not literally—this is fiction, after all. But it's where the novel happened in my head. And once the geographic specificity was pointed out to me, it made perfect sense.

I've always been a believer in something I've come to call "personal geography" (or, if I'm feeling lofty, "psychic geography"). There may be some arcane science that goes by that term, but I use it to refer to the way we reflexively and subconsciously build maps in our own head.

Note the plural: maps.

Take me, for instance. Anyone can log into GoogleMaps and pull up a map of Victoria and have a pretty clear, if abstract, sense of how the city is laid out. That's cartography. At a personal level, though: I've lived in Victoria for more than twenty years now; there are parts of the city I know very well, and parts that are a complete mystery. My personal map of the city, therefore, has incredibly detailed portions (downtown, Fernwood), and some areas that are barely more detailed than a street-map (Oak Bay, Gordon Head).

Picture one of those old encyclopedias, with the sections of transparencies to illustrate, say, human anatomy.

The cartographic map of Victoria is the base sheet, carefully labelled, and filed with the National Geographic or whatever society keeps track of these things, all grids and conspicuous landmarks (the Legislature, the Empress Hotel). Personal geography is the stack of transparent sheets that overlay that base sheet. The first one is knowledge: the sheet slides into place and certain areas of town go dark, and others become cluttered with landmarks.

And the next level, the next transparency sheet, is experience. In those bright, landmark-dotted areas of the map, there start to appear footnotes, memories. Beacon Hill Park where, during Luminara, I walked around in the gathering dark smoking a cigar and being part of a family-friendly group hallucination as powerful as any drug I've ever taken. The corner of Government and Yates, where I spent seven years working in a bookstore and where there's a Starbucks now (a Starbucks where my best friend—and former co-worker—and I insist on having a coffee whenever he's in town from Toronto, a bit of Venti-sized grave-dancing). The various stores—Munro's Books, Curious Comics—where I've spent too much time and money over the years. And then there are the missing places, sites that have disappeared but still occupy the personal map: that building will always be A&B Sound to me, no matter who takes it over. That building was the glass-blowing studio where Xander spent so many enthralled hours before they closed up shop. The restaurant where I interviewed Susan Musgrave, that's now a different restaurant where I've never been. The first bar I ever went to when I was legal, which is now a strip club, where I . . . nevermind. Ad infinitum.

This isn't a radical thought at all: everyone has their own personal geography of the places they know. My Victoria is my own, an image shaped from my experiences and my interests. I can tell you, for example, where every bookstore—used or new—is downtown, but I haven't the faintest idea of where one could buy shoes. I know where to find the best prices and selection on CDs, but I'd have to look up a men's clothing store in the phone book. Or stumble across it by accident. That's the "personal" part of personal geography; we all create our own cities around us.

But there's one page of transparency left. And as it slowly drifts into place, certain points on the map spark with an electrical current. Places I might not have even known I knew existed, or attached no particular memory to, crackle off the page.

The last transparency sheet? Resonance.

The funny thing about resonance—in general, I mean— is that you never know when it's going to hit, or just how hard it's going to hit you. That's why you can hear a song a thousand times, but when the circumstances are just right, the opening notes take you back, body and soul, to being in a car on the highway, watching a beautiful girl sing along, knowing with a gut-clenching certainty that there's more to this new relationship than meets the eye. That's why the smell of baking bread and cinnamon opens a door to a kitchen full of family, laughing and joking and eating, with no idea of the sadness that will inevitably come to them. That's why the touch of a certain breeze can transport you to a west shore beach, the feeling of wet socks and the laughter as a little boy looks for fossils in the rocks, and that's why the sound of Glenn Gould playing Bach's *Goldberg Variations* will always be the sound of falling in love. Resonance is the ghosts that haunt us, always present, whether we're aware of them in the moment or not.

Resonance is where, for me, the writing happens, geographically speaking.

Take *Before I Wake*, for example. The novel opens with a car accident, a hit-and-run, in a crosswalk near Hillside Mall. That crosswalk was part of the "knowledge"and "experience" levels of my personal geography: I used it every morning on my walk to work to cross the six lanes of traffic separating me from the bookstore. And the cars would whip through, regardless of who might be in the process of violating their God-given right to arrive at work as fast as possible, pedestrians be damned. The close calls, and the fear, gave that crosswalk resonance. When I needed a place for the hit-and-run to happen, well, there it was.

Similarly, Royal Jubilee Hospital. After the accident, Sherry is taken to RJH, and her parents spend a long time in the Emergency Room. Been there, done that. RJH is part of my knowledge, and part of my experience. The resonance, though, came from a very long afternoon in the ER when my wife was suffering a kidney stone attack a few years before I wrote the novel. I channelled the whole thing into the novel, not just the physical particulars, but the sense of helplessness that comes, that freakish distending of time that only occurs in hospital waiting rooms. And the resonance, it turns out, led me astray: RJH doesn't treat children. A little girl hit by a car would have been taken by ambulance out of town to Victoria General for treatment. Accuracy be damned, though: it's the resonance that matters.

And now that I'm aware of it, it's easy to see that that resonance, and my underlying interest in the physical place of my writing, has continued. My forthcoming novel, for example, is also set largely in Victoria. Thus, there's a musty, cluttered, antiquarian bookstore en route to downtown that plays a significant role in the book: Poor Richard's may be long gone from the actual map, but it lives on in my soul and, as Prospero's Books, in my work. And it's not just Victoria: there is a scene in the Astor Court, the gorgeous Zen scholar's garden in the Metropolitan Museum of Art in New York, and something terrible happens in a Portland hotel room. Well, the Astor Court is perhaps one of my favourite places on Earth. And I've stayed in that very hotel room. Resonances. Always resonances.

(As an aside, there is something interesting about resonance, I've discovered: it's cyclical. The act of writing about a place renders that place resonant, even if it wasn't prior to the act of getting it down on the page. Thus, walking around downtown Victoria is, these days, often a little surreal, with places given additional weight through their writing. And writing tends to fix those places, permanently, in my mind. Thus I'm surprised whenever I'm at RJH to discover that it has a sleek, modern ER, not the cracked, dingy hell-hole that I have in my memory, my soul, my book. And the library hasn't looked like it does in *Before I Wake* since before the novel came out. Often, walking through these familiar places feels like walking through a dream, or a dissociative state. It's like I don't know quite what's real, and what's not. Which, now that I think about it, is pretty much how I spend every waking moment, so . . . no harm there.)

My sense of place, and its importance, is perhaps closer to the surface when it comes to Henderson, the setting of *The World More Full of Weeping*, though the issues are a little cloudier. Actually, a lot cloudier.

A little background to start: I spent the first seventeen and a half years of my life in Agassiz, BC. Fourth generation.

The joke in Agassiz is that there are people *from* there, and newcomers. The dividing line is the flood: your family was here before the flood, or you're a newcomer. Of course, the flood occurred in 1948, which might give a sense of the Agassiz mindset. A skewed one, but a sense nonetheless.

(Another aside: it just occurred to me that I grew up in the distant shadow of the flood of '48, and with the annual awareness of the river rising against the dikes. Is it any wonder, given the universality of floods in world mythology, that I gravitated to a mythic interest? Things to ponder . . .)

Agassiz, at the time I was growing up, was home to about 3,500 people. A very small town. I had a wonderful and terrible childhood and adolescence; how I characterize it typically depends on what mood I'm in when I'm asked. Right now, I'm feeling a cautious warmth toward the world (it's 5:44 A.M., the sun is coming up, and the coffee is kicking in), so I can say that, despite the bullying and the pain and anguish that came with chunks of my teenage years, I had a pretty good childhood. I remember being outside all the time, riding my banana-seat bike in the driveway with my brothers, playing with the kids down the road, exploring the woods . . .

The woods.

Always the woods.

Here's the thing: Henderson is not Agassiz. Agassiz is not Henderson. I just want to be clear from the outset.

I mean, look at it objectively, side by side.

First: Agassiz is a small town in southwestern British Columbia, a farm-town nestled in a crook of the Fraser River about an hour and a half outside of Vancouver. A couple of days each year the air is so heavy with the smell of fertilizer from the fields that you almost taste the cow shit. Coming into town, you cross a bridge over the Fraser (which terrified me as a child, and terrifies me more now), you drive down either the front street or the back street. There's one high school, and in the mid-'80s a close group of friends won the Provincial basketball championships against all odds. There's a library, and a couple of coffee-shops, and down the road a piece is another little town, Harrison Hot Springs, on the shores of Harrison Lake. Every year in Agassiz, there's the Fall Fair and Corn Festival (third weekend in September), and the Corn King is crowned. The town is ringed with farms, and forests, and lazy back roads.

Okay, now Henderson.

Henderson is a small town in southwestern British Columbia, a farm-town nestled in a crook of a river about an hour and a half outside of Vancouver. A couple of days each year the air is so heavy with the smell of fertilizer from the fields that you almost taste the cow shit. Coming into town, you cross a bridge over the river, and you drive down either the front street or the back street. There's one high school, and in the mid-'80s a close group of friends won the Provincial basketball championships against all odds. There's a library, and a couple of coffee-shops, and down the road a piece is another little town, on the shores of a large, mysterious lake. Every year in Henderson, there's the Harvest Festival (third weekend in September), and the Harvest King is crowned. The town is ringed with farms, and forests, and lazy back roads. Oh, and it has a movie theatre.

See? Completely and utterly different. (Note the movie theatre.)

I'm not being facetious. Or coy. Agassiz is not Henderson.

The trick, even to my mind, is to balance the "is not"

with the fact that, at some levels, it "is."

With so many of my formative years spent in that small spot on the map, Agassiz is a wealth of memories and experiences. It's a veritable mine-field of resonance. Walking down the highway from the house where I grew up to my grandmother's house alone layers memory upon memory, some pleasant, some not so much. The smell of the dust on that road in high summer is almost crippling in the sheer amount of resonance it carries. That half mile stretch alone has enough in it for a book. Or two. The dusty air is thick with ghosts. And everywhere I turn in Agassiz, there's more, and more, and more. The past (Pang's restaurant, for example, where I lived every weekend for several years, drinking coffee and eating wonton soup and writing, always writing, while my girlfriend waited tables) jockeys for position with the present reality (that building burned down, for example, about a year ago). It's an absolute wealth of raw material, of emotion and memory and questions. . . .

To the point where I *can't* write about Agassiz. I simply can't.

And yet, I do. But I don't. (Are you starting to see how this works, in my head? Welcome to my head, by the way— it's a bit of a scary place.)

Writers have their places, locales and sites that inspire them, that give them homes and give them stories. James Joyce had Dublin, and he was unrepentant about it. On Bloomsday every year (which is, as I'm writing this, today, as a matter of fact), devotees gather to follow the steps of

Leopold Bloom through Dublin and through *Ulysses*. An entire industry has grown up around a single book and its fidelity to its sense of place (which is even more impressive, considering the novel was written in Switzerland, not Ireland, but I digress . . .). To a much lesser degree (because hey, we *are* talking Joyce here), I have Victoria. Walking tours could, conceivably, be led from location to location: Hillside Mall, Royal Jubilee, John's Place, the cliffs off Dallas Road, Pagliacci's. Okay, it's a much less interesting tour that Joyce's Dublin, but it could be done (and I suspect that, hard though it may be to believe, there may actually be more drinking involved in my tour than any Bloomsday ramble).

But I also have Agassiz. There are stories to tell, not of the town itself, but of some of the ideas around the town, some of the resonances. For better or worse, it inspires me, in ways that are at once inextricably linked to the physical place and simultaneously completely unrelated.

I'm not alone in this. Look at William Faulkner. He referred to Yoknapatawpha County as his "apocryphal county," based loosely on Lafayette County where he lived. Similarly, Manawaka, Manitoba was based loosely on Neepawa, Margaret Laurence's hometown. And look at Stephen King, whose Derry and Castle Rock are clearly more than inspired by the small Maine towns he knows so well.

The question then, I suppose, is why? To get all rhetorical and third-person-y about it: if you're going to write about a place, and you've gone on at great length to clarify just how important the place is to you and your writing, why not just write about the place? For the love of God, man, why tie yourself up in knots over it?

And the only way I can answer is to repeat myself: because Henderson is not Agassiz. Except inasmuch as it is.

An anecdote might help.

Henderson was born in the early 1990s, on the main floor of the Book Warehouse store on Broadway in Vancouver. It was the third week of September. I was managing the Book Warehouse location in Victoria at that point, and I was working for a week at the flagship store, connecting with the head office, getting to know how things were done in the big city. It was a Friday afternoon. I had come back from lunch at a little Chinese restaurant a couple of doors down (wonton soup, naturally), and I was feeling the first buzzes of an MSG reaction when one of the people working there asked me what I was doing for the weekend.

So I explained that my wife was coming over from Victoria and we were headed out to Agassiz for the Fall Fair that afternoon.

The Agassiz Fall Fair is a big deal in the way that only smalltown fall fairs can be a big deal. It's the equivalent of homecoming weekend at your better universities: everybody who can come back, comes back. It's a celebration of friends and family, an annual opportunity to re-connect with one's roots. This person I was talking to didn't know that, however, so I had to explain the Fall Fair in detail. And after I described the rides and the judging of preserves and baking and crafts and the beer garden and how much

I missed the old days of the demolition derby, I explained about the crowning of the Corn King.

"It's pretty prestigious," I explained. "All the local farmers who are growing corn that year are entered, and their fields and their crops are evaluated by a panel of experts, people from the Experimental Farm, that sort of thing. And the one with the finest crop is crowned the Corn King. There's a robe and a crown and everything."

And that's the whole story. That's what the Corn King is, more or less (if I were inclined to research further, I would know exactly who to call—one of the benefits of smalltown life). Except I didn't stop there. And to this day, I don't know where the next comment came from, or how it came to me. But came it did.

"And then," I continued, completely deadpan, "at midnight he's sacrificed to the Old Gods to ensure a plentiful harvest for the next year."

She laughed (of course it was a she); it wasn't bad as far as punchlines go.

I didn't laugh. And in that moment, my life changed, and Henderson was born.

Because all that stuff about the Fall Fair, the homecoming, the crowning of the Corn King? That's all Agassiz.

The mythic, ritual, pagan sacrifice of the Corn King for the benefit of the community, though? That's Henderson. There are any number of perfectly valid reasons to create a mirror-image of an existing community to use as a location for one's writing. Hell, I subscribe to any number of perfectly straightforward reasons to justify my having done it.

Chief among these is likely practicality. Simply put, it's easier to write about a place that you're making up because you can include what you need. When you're writing based in and on a real place, you're pretty much limited to the existing reality. Yeah, I said pretty much; I haven't always followed that rule, as my mentions of Sherry being treated at Royal Jubilee in *Before I Wake* and the continued existence of an antiquarian bookstore in the new novel where now there is only a financial planning company should attest. As a general rule, though, inventing a place gives you more freedom. I couldn't, for example, write about characters in Agassiz going to a movie, because Agassiz, during the time of my existence hasn't had a movie theatre. Henderson does, though. (Can you tell I'm still a little ticked at the lack of a movie theatre in Agassiz when I was growing up?) It allows you a larger freedom as well, the freedom to create histories and identities and backstories. Again, if you need it, you can create it. It's not like writing about Victoria and needing, for some reason, to have the city destroyed in a historic fire at the turn of the century. That kind of thing just doesn't fly.

And then there's the issue of . . . well, let's call it civility. But fear might be another way of looking at it. And deniability. Let's face it, if you're writing in the "real" world, somebody, somewhere, sometime is going to get pissed and assume that the very worst of the characters in your book is, in fact, a barely concealed version of his- or herself. Nobody wants a story filled with saints and piety (God, where would be the fun in that?), but people don't want to think that they're the basis for the very nadir of your creations. And in the event that you're confronted by a 6' 2" refrigerator of a man with a badge, who's drunkenly complaining that the pants-wetting, alcoholic, child-molesting deputy in your book must be him, being able to say, "No, no, it's just a story! See! It's in a completely different town! Completely imaginary!" might, just might, help you avoid the shit-kicking, which, let's face it, you probably deserve.

I'm sure the residents of Lafayette County and Neepawa weren't always that keen on how "they" were depicted in Faulkner and Laurence's writing, but what can you do?

And speaking of shit-kicking, there's also the issue of cruelty. And this is, for me, a pretty pertinent reason to distance a real town by creating a simulacrum.

Let's look at Castle Rock and Derry, two of Stephen King's "wholesome" little towns. Jesus, what that man puts those people through is nothing short of malicious. I mean, killer clowns, fer the love of Pete! Does it get any worse than that? And I bet he does it with a smile on his face. No, I'm sure he does it with a smile on his face, because I've been there. I've done that. The things that happen in the Henderson stories . . . the mind reels.

And while the thought of burning the town of Agassiz to the ground is reprehensible (and, yes, I realize, likely psychotic), with Henderson, it's all right. No, it's better than all right: it's the right thing to do. Well, given the context and the events surrounding it.

Which is probably the key thing, now that I think about it. The main reason for the creation of Henderson was that it allowed me access to those stories I wanted to tell, and a context in which to tell them.

Let's face it—I'm odd. I know that. Anyone who's spent any time at all talking with me knows it; it's an undeniable fact.

And I have odd ideas for stories. How else would I be able to go from a perfectly innocent, nay, almost heart-warming story about a smalltown agricultural fair to a story that has its roots in ideas of pagan sacrifice, the Eleusinian Mysteries and a willing death for the good of a community? That's not a logical leap.

And so long as I was thinking about Agassiz, it was an impossible leap even for me to make.

Agassiz is so rich in my mind, its people so familiar to me, its landscape so real, so drenched in memory and experience, that it's literally impossible for me to write about it. And certainly impossible for me to turn the full, and more than occasionally destructive, force of my imagination on it.

Turn it one degree toward the weird, though, and not only can I turn my imagination on it, but I do. With relish.

Or, to put it another way (and to deliver the pay-off for the analogy I established earlier):

Imagine a stack of transparency sheets overlaying a strict, cartographical rendering of the town of Agassiz, and its surrounding forests and hills and cemeteries and lakeshore. Look at the whole stack: the cartographical base; the knowledge transparency, with my deep, intimate awareness of the town; the experience transparency, with seventeen years worth of memories (and, let's face it, baggage); and finally, the resonance level, with the darkness of my imagination and the brightness of my ghosts.

That, right there, is my Agassiz you're holding in your hands. My personal geography, in one possibly over-developed metaphor.

Now, grab the top transparency, the resonance sheet, and fold it carefully back while you tear out the other two transparencies—knowledge and experience—and toss them in the nearest trash can (or, if you're feeling symbolic, set them aflame with a Zippo lighter). Now, take out a Sharpie, scribble over the name "Agassiz" on the base sheet and scrawl in the name "Henderson." And finally, let the only remaining transparency sheet fall back into place: resonance on top of cartography, divorced from knowledge and experience.

That's Henderson, right there. One degree of weird— and an entire universe—away from Agassiz.

Or, as I've always maintained (and if you want to go all quantum for your metaphors), two very real towns, occupying the same very real space, but in parallel universes.

The creation of Henderson (or discovery, really, because I suppose it was always there somewhere, in the depths of my subconscious) allowed me to create, not quite out of whole cloth, a history for the town. A population. A dynamic and a psyche.

It allowed me to create a world.

And over the last decade and a half, through a dozen or so short stories, a novella or two, and a shortish, abandoned novel, I've developed that world with a level of detail and immersion the extent of which I don't think I'm even aware of yet. I know where everything is in Henderson, how settings relate to settings not in the abstract but at a level of roads and paths through fields and forests. I know the history of Henderson. I know its people, and who they relate to, and how.

You've met a few of them now. Some of them you'll see again, in the way that you'll always run into people you know in a small town. Especially when they're as significant to the town and its history as John Joseph and his wife Claire. You'll hear about the flood of '49. And the year the town burned to the ground, following an endless summer of madness and violence and no rain. You'll hear stories of birth, and of death, and of myths alive and walking the backroads and paths.

And forests. Can't forget the forests.

Did I say "flood" up there? Ah, yes, so I did. Yes, Henderson has a flood. Much like Agassiz did, sixty plus years ago. Things happen like that in the weird relationship between the two places. Events and locations shift amorphously from one reality to the next. Take the woods in *The World More Full of Weeping*: I know those woods. I've walked those woods. When I was Brian's age, I thought about disappearing into them.

And last June, during a long-weekend family reunion,

I walked into them again. Not far, because they scare me as much as they attract me. But far enough to really feel them again, to be reminded that they were as I had both imagined and remembered.

Because the woods in *The World More Full of Weeping* are the ones at the back of my grandmother's house, the house where, in the novella, Brian and his father live.

It's funny, though: walking through Agassiz, spending the weekend in the house where I grew up (which is the house in "The Small Rain Down," for the record), I didn't feel any of the surreality that accompanies me so often in Victoria. In my grandmother's house, I was surrounded by my family—there wasn't the slightest sense of being in two places at once, or having my real life and the life I had created for Brian and Jeff awkwardly juxtaposed.

That's the main thing about Henderson: it's utterly fictional, even though it might seem otherwise. And therefore I can breathe easy.

Stepping into the woods, though . . .

Stepping into the woods was like crossing a threshold, from the heat of the day to the cool of the shadows. From the noise of the fifty or sixty family members in the backyard preparing for a group photograph to the not-quite-stillness, the slow, steady hum of mystery and life unfolding unseen all around me.

It was as if, in one step, I went from Agassiz to Henderson. By entering the woods, I had moved between worlds.

Which I suppose is the last word. Because that's what happens when you walk into the woods.

ACKNOWLEDGEMENTS

To get it out of the way at the start: any credit goes to others. Blame, however, comes straight to me.

As always, a writer is grateful to his readers, and I'm no exception. I'm most grateful to those readers who get the story first, hot and pulpy and fresh, whose eyes help shape it into even a modicum of respectability. For these stories, my deepest gratitude to James Grainger and to Colin Holt, fine readers and fine friends both (even when I don't pull my own weight). And Colin deserves extra thanks, for all his help—above and beyond the call of duty, my friend.

I would also like to thank the readers on the RWF Yahoo board. It's a strange world where a group of Springsteen fans can come together as first readers and fiction enablers, but it's a world I'm delighted to live in. Thanks, then, to Ruth, Adam, Fredo, Michael, Kathryn, Ray and Karen. And to Laurie and Matthias, who also weighed in. Strange how easily strangers can become friends without even meeting.

Random House Canada was very gracious in allowing this slim volume to sneak out—my thanks to my publisher, Anne Collins, for her understanding, and to my agent, Anne McDermid, for facilitating the whole process.

Most times you can't judge a book by its cover. In this case, however, I just hope the book even approaches the sheer brilliance of the cover that Erik Mohr created for it. I stand in awe.

My deepest gratitude to Brett Alexander Savory and his partner-in-crime Sandra Kasturi at ChiZine—just two crazy kids with a dream! Working with Brett has been a treat, a reminder of times—which may not have actually existed—when book deals were made over pints of beer. . . . Let not that casualness fool you, though: Brett and Sandra are the epitome of professionalism, as the beauty of this book well attests.

And finally, immeasurable thanks to the home team. Xander is the greatest kid in the world, and very understanding of the hard work and occasional sacrifices required to make this writing life work. And Cori . . . I cannot thank you enough. Your faith sustains me, your questions galvanize me, and your response to any story is the one that matters most. A writer could not ask for a finer first reader, a fiercer first critic, or a more supportive partner.

ABOUT THE AUTHOR

ROBERT J. WIERSEMA

Robert J. Wiersema is a bookseller and reviewer, who contributes regularly to the *Vancouver Sun*, the *Globe and Mail*, the *Ottawa Citizen*, and numerous other newspapers. Wiersema is also the event coordinator for Bolen Books, and the author of *Before I Wake* (Random House Canada, 2006), which was a national bestseller. He lives in Victoria, B.C., with his wife, Cori Dusmann, and their son, Xander.